S0-BEF-346

Snug Harbor Stories

a WALLACE the BRAVE collection!

Will Henry

Andrews McMeel
PUBLISHING®

to my wife

MRS. MACINTOSH, HOW MANY DAYS LEFT IN SCHOOL?
TEN DAYS, WALLACE
GOLD STAR

TEN LAID-BACK, END-OF-THE-LINE, GLORIOUSLY UNPRODUCTIVE DAYS

TEN WHOLE DAYS ?!?
YOU CAN ALMOST SEE THE BEACH FROM HERE
Will Henry

CLASS, FOR OUR LAST ASSIGNMENT, I'D LIKE YOU TO WRITE DOWN ALL THE FUN THINGS YOU'LL BE DOING THIS SUMMER

WHIRRR

I DON'T HAVE THE VOCABULARY

C'MON, SPUD! LET'S GO TO THE BEACH!!
WHAT WAS I TOLD TO DO WHEN I CROSS A STREET?

I THINK IT WAS "STOP, LOOK AND LISTEN"

WAIT, NO, WAS IT "STOP, DROP AND ROLL"?

"NEVER WEAR WHITE AFTER LABOR DAY"?
Will "GwanPub" Henry

ahem

FOOD FIGHT!

PLIP.

I APPRECIATE THE SUPPORT, WALLACE
YOU WERE DYING UP THERE
PRINCIP

BOYS, THAT'S DEFINITELY ENOUGH VIDEO GAMES FOR TONIGHT
Chop. Chop

BOYS?

yessssss, mother

DON'T GO UPSTAIRS
Will Henry

HELLO, SPUD
HI, MRS. McCLELLAN!

WALLACE ISN'T HOME FROM PRACTICE YET
I KNOW, I CAME TO GRAB A SNACK

A SNACK ???
WALLACE SAID IT WAS **OK**
Will Henry

HE **DID**?
YOU NEED TO START GETTING RANCH IN BULK
Will Henry

I'M GLAD YOU JOINED MY SASQUATCH EXPEDITION!
WELL, I WAS SITTING IN MY FAVORITE NOOK WHEN MY MOTHER COMES IN AND GOES-

SPUD! YOU NEED TO GO OUTSIDE AND GET SOME FRESH AIR!
SAFETY FIRST
Will Henry

SWEET
HAS THE SUN ALWAYS BEEN THIS BRIGHT?

DAD, DO YOU HAFTA WORK TODAY?
OF COURSE, WALLACE

I'M WONDERING BECAUSE I'M ON SUMMER BREAK AND LEGITIMATELY HAVE NOTHING TO DO BUT GO TO THE BEACH
Will Henry

HAVE FUN AT WORK, THOUGH

A LITTLE TASTE OF YOUR OWN MEDICINE
WHAT HAVE I CREATED?

YOU CATCH ANY-THING COOL, AMELIA?
OBVIOUSLY
William Henry

LET'S SEE, I'VE GOT TWO GRASSHOPPERS, A CRICKET, A WORM, A FEW BEETLES AND...

ONE LEGIT TOAD!
WOW
EW

HAVE YOU TRIED TO KISS IT YET?
HEH, LIKE I NEED A PRINCE

MOM LOOK! LOOK MOM
OVER HERE LOOK LOOK
LOOK MOM WHY AREN'T
YOU LOOKING MOM
MOM MOM
LOOK!

WHAT CAN I GET YOU FOLKS?
SMALL VANILLA
VANILLA?

DUDE, VANILLA IS BORING
IT IS BORING
IT'S CLASSIC
I WANT OREO

GRASSHOPPER
ONE GRASS-HOPPER
NO
OR COOKIE DOUGH

NO NO, SORRY, HE WANTS, LIKE, REAL GRASSHOPPERS
eck GROSS
MINT CHIP?

WHAT? IT'S A PHASE... WALLACE, WHAT FLAVOR?
I BET
ummm...

I GOT A LINE FORMING, LADY
WALLACE, MAKE UP YOUR MIND
DEFINITELY MOOSETRACKS

FINE, ONE MOOSE-TRACKS, ONE-
NO WAIT!

GAHH! YOU'RE ALL GETTING VANILLA!!!

AMELIA, YOU WANNA HELP US FIND A SASQUATCH?
WALLACE, PLEASE
YOU CAN'T FIND A SASQUATCH...

SASQUATCH FINDS YOU!
OH, THEN THIS WILL BE EASY
Will Henry

IF WE'RE GONNA CATCH A SASQUATCH, WE'LL NEED BERRIES
W. Hency

AS BAIT?
NO.

Squish

WAR PAINT
OR HIVES

I AM WALLACE...
THE BRAVE
I AM SPUD...
ALONG FOR THE RIDE
AND I AM
AMELIA...
Will Henry

TAKER OF
SOULS!!!

SCIENTISTS SAY A SASQUATCH CAN MORPH INTO OTHER SHAPES...

ROCKS, BUSHES, STUMPS, ANIMALS, ANYTHING!
Will Hendg

HECK, SPUD'S MOM COULD BE A SASQUATCH
IT WOULD EXPLAIN THE HAIR

HOW **TALL** DO SASQUATCHES GET?
PRETTY TALL

CLICK
Will Henry

EVERYBODY HAS SEEN THAT PHOTO, RIGHT?
SUDDENLY, I FEEL LIKE A CHICKEN NUGGET

I KINDA HOPE WE DON'T FIND A SASQUATCH
ARE YOU KIDDING?!? IF WE CAPTURED A SASQUATCH...

LINE STARTS HERE!
Amelia Presents BIGFOOT
$$$$
Will Henry

I'D BE FILTHY RICH!
CATCH AND RELEASE ONLY

BINGO! THIS IS UNMISTAKABLY A SASQUATCH CLEARING!!
W.H.

THE SASQUATCH LAID RIGHT HERE, PLAYING A UKULELE FOR ITS WOODLAND FRIENDS AS THEY WATCHED THE STARS COME OUT

sighhh... WE NEED TO BE MORE LIKE THE SASQUATCH
STORED ITS BACON-WAVE HERE

THIS IS BORING
WE **WILL** FIND A SASQUATCH, AMELIA

WALLACE, THE SASQUATCH DON'T LIVE HERE, THEY LIVE IN THE PACIFIC NORTHWEST!
SAYS WHO?!

THE GOVERNMENT ???
BECAUSE THEIR DIET CONSISTS OF **TREE FROGS** AND **HIPSTERS**
Will Hency

THIS IS STILL BORING!
I'VE GOT A WAGON

WE CAN SET UP A RAMP AND TRY TO LAUNCH OUTTA THE STRATOSPHERE
ZOOM!!
Will Henry

IT'S THE QUICKEST WAY TO BECOME AN ASTRONAUT
I HATED SPACE CAMP...

WHAT'S THE NEXT PAINFULLY BORING PLAN?
OH...

...SWEET...
Will Henry

...NEPTUNE!

WALLACE, THIS IS A BOX OF JUNK
FREE JUNK!
FREE SHTUFF!

THIS IS A LEGITIMATE BOX OF GARBAGE
SPUD, ANYTHING COULD BE IN THIS BOX!
FREE

BASEBALL CARDS, COMIC BOOKS, BEACH BALLS!
Will Henry

...PHOTON PHASERS, TRANSMOGRIFIERS
CURSED MEDALLIONS, OLD UNDERPANTS
MY WASTED MORNING

JACKPOT BABY!
WHAT IS IT?
FREE

THIS, AMELIA, IS A LAVA LAMP!
bingo

I'VE HEARD OF THESE THINGS

A RELIC OF A FORGOTTEN SOCIETY
FORGOTTEN OR DESTROYED BY LAVA?
WillHenry

SO, WHAT DOES THIS DINKY LAVA LAMP DO?
IT'S AMAZING

IMAGINE TWO SUPER-CHARGED GALAXIES COLLIDING, CREATING A LIGHT SHOW SO SURREAL, IT'S MATCHED ONLY BY THE BRILLIANCE OF THE COSMOS!
Will Henry
BOOM

ALL CONFINED IN YOUR LIVING ROOM
THING MUST REALLY POP WHEN YOU PLUG IT IN

DO YOU GUYS WANNA PLAY CAPTURE THE FLAG?

WE WOULD, BUT...

!
!

A FIREFLY GOT STUCK UP MY NOSE
TWO NIGHTS AGO!

WALLACE, DO YOU AND YOUR FRIENDS WANT LUNCH?
I DUNNO, WE'RE IN THE MIDDLE OF
WAIT!

huff huff

huff huff huff huff

DID huff DID SOMEONE SAY "LUNCH"?
SUCH RAW ATHLETICISM

DID YOU MAKE PEANUT BUTTER AND JELLY?
I DID

DID YOU ADD BANANA SLICES?
I DID

AND A HANDFUL OF CEREAL FOR CRUNCH
Will "Captin Crunch" Henry

WE ARE GROOVIN', MOM
WE ARE
I DEMAND TO BE GROOVIN' !!!

DO YOU THINK DAD WILL LET ME BUILD A CLUBHOUSE IN THE SHED ?
ONLY IF YOU INVITE YOUR BROTHER

STERLING? HOW COME?!

BECAUSE...
Will Henry

I HAVE TO GET HIM OUTTA THE HOUSE
i'm touching your face!!
grumble

DAD, CAN WE USE THE SHED AS OUR CLUBHOUSE?
WHAT'RE YOU KIDS GONNA DO IN THERE?

munch
WE'RE JUST...

WE'RE GONNA TRY TO MAKE THE WORLD A BETTER PLACE
FEELS LIKE I'M WITNESSING HISTORY
Will Henry

OK, WALLACE, YOU CAN USE THE SHED AS A CLUBHOUSE
YAHS!

FIRST ORDER OF BUSINESS, ADD A BALL PIT, WALL-TO-WALL!!
THEN, BOOM, ZIPLINE STRAIGHT INTO THE OCEAN!
Will Henry

LET'S START WITH A SHELF TO PUT YOUR STUFF ON
YOU OLD PEOPLE MOVE SO SLOWWW!

WE SHOULD MAKE A CLUB-HOUSE IN MY SHED
AND HAVE A GRAND **LAVA LAMP** VIEWING PARTY!
OH LEMME GUESS
Will Henry

GIRLS AREN'T ALLOWED
NO NO NO NO NOooo
GIRLS ARE ENCOURAGED
DO YOU **WANT** THE NICKNAME "ONE THUMB"?

YOU KIDS FOUND A LAVA LAMP, HUH?

I HAD ONE OF THOSE IN MY DORM, SEE
Will Hensy

U.R.I. → '92
I USED TO BE "RAD" BEFORE I WAS "DAD"
WAS THIS A HALLOWEEN PARTY?

AND NOW, THE MAIN EVENT!
CLIK

WHHHOOAAAA!!!
W.Henry

hello.

THERE WAS A TIME EVERYBODY HAD A LAVA LAMP...

THEN ALL OF A SUDDEN SNAP
THEY WENT OUT OF STYLE
Will Henry

BECAUSE KEEPING A JAR OF LAVA IN YOUR HOUSE IS DANGEROUS!!
DANGEROUS NEVER GOES OUTTA STYLE

WAAALLACE, DINNER!!!
SWEET! YOU GUYS WANT BURGERS?
CLUB HO
I WOULD LOVE A BURGER, BUT MY MOTHER WON'T LET ME EAT RED MEAT
Will Henry

EVERYTHING WE EAT TASTES LIKE A PIECE OF WET CARD-BOARD!
YOU ARE WHAT YOU EAT...
I CAN SEE IT

WALLACE, WOULD YOU LIKE A HOT DOG, A BURGER OR SOMETHING ELSE?

Will Henry

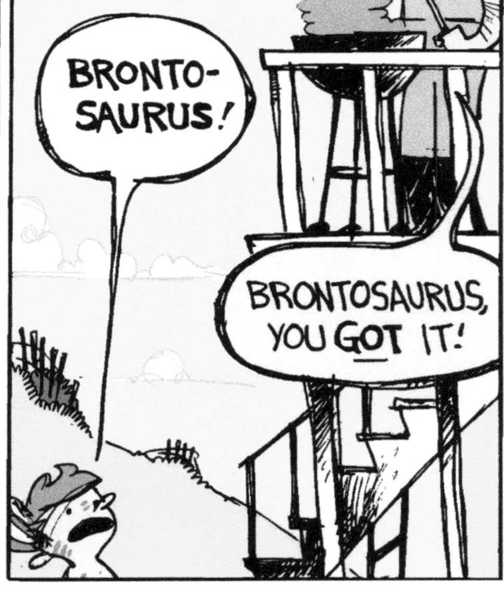
BRONTO-SAURUS!
BRONTOSAURUS, YOU GOT IT!

WHATCHA DOIN', WALLACE?
ENJOYING THE SUN-SHINE, SPUD

oh

Will Henry

I THINK MY MOTHER IS GOING TO SELL ME FOR GROCERY COUPONS
NOT TODAY, SPUD

NOW LOOKY HERE! I'M QUICK DRAW!

THA DEADLIEST COWBOY IN DER WEST !!!

AND MAH HEART IS AS **BLACK** AS MY PEPPERY INSIDES!!
YOU JUS' WAIT RAGHT THER', QUICK DRAW!

I'M THA' SHERIFF ROUN' THESE HERE PARTS!
!

AND I DON' LIKE YER ATTITUDE!

GAH! i'm mr. salt and my head popped off!!!
?

?
my guts are spilling EVERYWHERE!
oh the humanity

'SCUSE ME!

PLEASE DON'T WASTE THE SALT
STERLING!
QUICK DRAW RIDES THE NAPKIN HOLDER INTO THE SUNSET
-menu-

WHOA, MOM!
Will Henry

LOOK HOW HAIRY THIS GUY'S LEGS ARE !!!

APOLOGIES
?
FEELS LIKE A DOG

FOR MY FIRST PICK, I'LL TAKE AMELIA!!!
NICE
HA! YOUR FIRST PICK FOR A WATER-BALLOON FIGHT IS A GIRL?!?

SLAP
!

I LIKE YA, KEVIN, BUT I CAN'T HELP YOU NOW
HERE, CALL YOUR MOTHER

sting

YOWIE

A BEE! I STEPPED ON A STUPID BEE!!!

THE ONE TIME I GO BAREFOOT!
WHAT'S A BEE DOIN' ON THE GROUND ANYWAY?!
I HATE BEES
I'LL NEVER EAT HONEY AGAIN!

YOU ALRIGHT, LITTLE GUY?
bzzz

I DROPPED MY SMART-PHONE YESTERDAY AND IT BROKE
The NARWH
~Snug Harbor

MY MOTHER WON'T BUY ME A NEW ONE, AND I HAVE **NO** IDEA WHY...
YOU HAVE NO IDEA WHY?

HERE, HOLD THIS ROCK
NO IDEA...
The NARWH
~Snug Harbo

SLIP
The NARWH
~Snug Harbo

The NARWHA
~snug Harbor

BONK
PLIP

The NARWH
~snug Harbor

POINT TAKEN
The NARW
~snug Harbor

YOU HEAR ABOUT JUSTIN McMAHON?
skip
zing

HE SKIPPED A ROCK SO HARD...

IT SKIPPED ALL THE WAY ACROSS THE ATLANTIC AND-
skip
skipperoo

skip
skip
BONK

HIT SOME OLD DUDE IN IRELAND
WE HAVE **GOT** TO GET HIM ON OUR BASEBALL TEAM
zing

WOULD YOU RATHER HAVE THE POWER OF FLIGHT OR INVISIBILITY?

DEFINITELY INVISIBILITY...

MOSTLY SO PEOPLE WOULDN'T BE ABLE TO TALK TO ME
Will Henry

YOU'RE **STILL** CATCHING BUTTERFLIES?
SPUD, IF EVERYTHING GOES TO PLAN...
I'LL BE IN **TAHITI** BY LUNCHTIME
I, **TOO**, LOOK FORWARD TO LUNCHTIME
munch
munch

HEY, SPUD, YOU DOIN' ANYTHING TONIGHT?
NO... NOT YET

I WAS GONNA SEE HOW CLOSE I CAN GET TO A SKUNK WITHOUT BEING SPRAYED
what?

I FIGURE I CAN SIT ON MY PICNIC TABLE AND LURE THEM IN WITH BREAD

YOU WANNA COME?
HA! WALLACE...

HOW DID
I GET
HERE?

MOM, I WANNA BE A FISHERMAN, LIKE DAD!
OH REALLY?

YEA! YOU GET TO EXPLORE THE SEVEN SEAS...

FIND LOST TREASURE...

AND FIGHT
SEA MONSTERS

YOU **MIGHT** BE ROMANTICIZING IT A BIT, WALLACE
HOW SO?

NARWHAL

KICK
KICK
KICK
KICK

Will Henry

IT'S THE LITTLE THINGS...
THAT DRIVE YOU NUTS

MOM, ARE YOU ALMOST **DONE** WITH MY COMIC BOOK ?
I NEED TO MAKE SURE IT'S APPROPRIATE FOR CHILDREN
William Henry

I WILL SAY, THERE'S A **CRAZY** TWIST AT THE END
SHWAPS

DO YOU WANNA KNOW WHAT IT IS ?
DON'T RUIN IT!
ruin it
SHWAPS

YOUR UNCLE WAS A BIG MAN
I HOPE I GET **BIGGER** SOMEDAY
Will Henry

BOY DID HE LIKE BONBONS
LIKE, "CALL THE NATIONAL **GUARD**" BIG!

THIS IS THE **BEST** FORT WE'VE EVER MADE!
AGREED

I DON'T KNOW WHY WE DIDN'T THINK OF THIS BEFORE
ALL IT TOOK WAS A BIG BED SHEET

Yy Zz
giggle
giggle
Billy Henry

I'M WORRIED MY HANDS AREN'T GROWING PROPORTIONATELY TO MY BODY

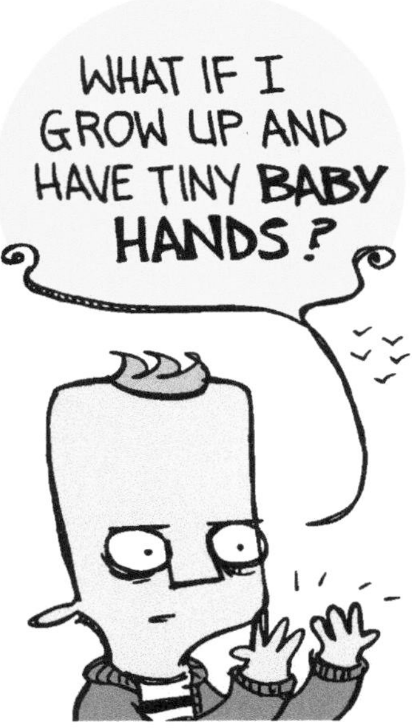
WHAT IF I GROW UP AND HAVE TINY **BABY HANDS**?

I WON'T BE ABLE TO GIVE HANDSHAKES OR PALM A BASKETBALL...
Will Henry

YOU DON'T **LIKE** BASKET-BALL
I'LL LOOK **FOOLISH** HOLDING GRAPE-FRUITS

I WISH MY PARENTS WOULD GET ME A PET
I HAD A PET... KINDA

EVERY NIGHT I COULD HEAR A STRAY CAT POKING AROUND OUR TRASH CANS

ONE NIGHT, I MUSTERED UP ENOUGH COURAGE TO TRY AND PET IT

LUCKY...
SKUNK
Will Henry

SO, GUIDE THE BASKETBALL WITH YOUR LEFT HAND AND **SHOOT** WITH YOUR RIGHT
OH, LIKE-

SO!

BWONG!

BWANG!

BWONG
BWANG

ANCHORS AWEIGH, BOYS!
BAP
VRRRR

toot
tooooot

BETTER...
I HIT THE BACKBOARD

THIS NEW **SHWAPS** PINBALL MACHINE IS ABSOLUTELY **INCREDIBLE**!
BANG
bing!
POP!

NOT ONLY IS SHWAPS MY **FAVORITE** SUPERHERO, BUT THIS CRAFTSMANSHIP IS **SUPERB**!
curse you, Shwaps
RIGHT ON, BRAH!
BOOM!
10
SHWAPS

IS IT POSSIBLE TO LOVE A MACHINE?
I DATED MY SMART-PHONE FOR A COUPLE WEEKS
smooch
W.Henry

WHAT'S GOING ON HERE?!
I BET WALLACE HE COULDN'T DO SEVENTY PUSH-UPS
Hngg

I TRIED TO DO A PUSHUP, ONCE
Hng

ENDED UP TAKING A RATHER PLEASANT NAP
Hngg
WHAT'S THE COUNT?
two
Will Henry

DAD, CAN YOU MAKE ME A PANCAKE TOP HAT ?
I DON'T QUITE UNDERSTAND

IT'S SIMPLE, REALLY. WITH A LITTLE SYRUP AND THE RIGHT SHAPED PANCAKES, YOU CAN CONSTRUCT A TOP HAT
Will Henry

STILL VERY, **VERY** CONFUSED
LEMME GET MY DIAGRAMS
PANCAKE MIX

EVERY YEAR MY MOM TAKES ME TO THE PUMPKIN PATCH AND I **HATE** IT

AND EVERY YEAR I "**HAVE**" TO TAKE A PICTURE NEXT TO THE ENORMOUS GOURD
Smile
Will Henry

I'VE ALWAYS WANTED TO PUSH THAT THING DOWN A HILL
WE'D BE DOOMED

:psst:: WALLACE, DO YOU HAVE THE ANSWER TO NUMBER FOUR?
what?

GUESS NOT
W.Henry

NOT MANY LOBSTERS IN THESE TRAPS, DAD
CASH 4 FISH
FISH

HAVE YOU TRIED POLITELY ASKING THE LOBSTERS TO SWIM INTO THE TRAPS?
Wee Willy Henry

IT'D BE A TOUGH SELL, WALLACE
LEAD WITH A JOKE

LOOK AT THIS HONKER OF A TREE
Will Henry

TO THINK IT ALL STARTED WITH A TEENY WEENY ACORN
AND GREW INTO SOMETHING AS INCREDIBLE AS THIS!
nice

IT'LL HAPPEN TO YOU SOMEDAY, WALLACE
I'M GONNA TURN INTO A TREE?

FOR MY SELF-PORTRAIT, I DREW MY-SELF WITH A **JETPACK**...
WALLACE!
Will Henry

THAT WAY I CAN FLY AROUND AND VISIT OTHER DRAWINGS
Jamie...
HOWDY
(hello)
HI
WALLACE!
SPUD
YO
SUP
HI
kerry
Ben

WALLACE! YOUR CLASSMATES WORKED HARD ON THOSE!
Eh, I PHONED IT IN

'SCUSE ME, MA'AM, I'M LOOKING FOR A BOOK
WHAT BOOK, SWEETIE?
Read

ONE OF THOSE BOOKS WHERE YOU OPEN IT UP AND RAINBOWS AND DRAGONS AND ALL THIS WEIRD STUFF STARTS SPEWING OUT
ZOOM

LIKE IN ALL THE COMMER-CIALS
WE HAVE **POP-UP** BOOKS
Read

SPUD!! MY DAD IS GONNA COACH BASKETBALL THIS YEAR!!
NO WAY!
WHICH MEANS WE'RE GONNA BE ON THE SAME TEAM!
YAS!

I CAN FINALLY WEAR MY BASKET-BALL HELMET
WRONG SPORT!
Will Henry

WHOA, WE SHOULDN'T GO THIS WAY
?

YOU SEE THAT GRUNGY OLD-TIMER?
THE DUDE WHO IS ALWAYS FISHING OFF THE BRIDGE?

HE'S NOT FISHING, WALLACE!

HE'S FEEDING A BUCKET OF SCUP HEADS TO THE HOBGOBLIN UNDER THE BRIDGE

THAT WAY THE BEAST DOESN'T GET HUNGRY AND START EATING THE TOWNSPEOPLE

THAT MAN IS THE UNSUNG HERO OF SNUG HARBOR
UNTIL **YOU** END UP IN THE BUCKET

HUN, I'M TAKING THE BOYS TO BASKETBALL!
Will Henry

I'M GOING TO SIT THIS ONE OUT
REALLY? WHAT'RE YOU GONNA DO?

nothing

I'M GOING TO DO NOTHING
LUCKY...

WALLACE, I'M DEFINITELY NOT AN ATHLETE
MORE OF A "MATHLETE"?

NOT EVEN!

I'M MORE OF A "BATHLETE"
Will Henry

I LOVE TAKING BATHS
HOPE YOU'RE BETTER AT IT

WHAT'S WITH THE CLIPBOARD?
OH, THIS CLIPBOARD?

YOUR DAD PUT IT ON MY HEAD AND WALKED AWAY
BRING IT IN

WHAT AN **ODD** COACHING STYLE
I WAS BORN FOR THIS POSITION
William Henry

THERE'S GONNA BE A SCREEN BY THE KEY...
Tweet

WALLACE, YOU COME AROUND LOOKING TO-
Tweet
tweet

Tweet
TWEET
Tweet
TWeet
tweet
WillHenry

WHO GAVE STERLING A WHISTLE?
i took it!!

Erf

HA
HA
HA
HAAAAAA!!
PAP PAP PAP PAP
PAP PAP PAP PAP
PAP
PAP
PAP PAP
Erf
Will Henry

Erf

PiP
Erf

Will Henry

TOUCH DOWN!!

SPUD, YOU SEE THIS?
THAT PUMPKIN WITH A HOLE IN THE BOTTOM ?

THIS IS MY **NEW**, TOTALLY RADICAL HALLOWEEN MASK
EW

'SCUSE ME WHILE I TERRORIZE THE VILLAGE
Will Henry

BONK!
THERE'S A **HOUSE** THERE!

DO NOT FEAR!!
IT'S ONLY ME UNDER THIS GHOULISH MASK
Hm?

WAIT, WHO'S UNDER THERE?
DAD! IT'S ME, WALLACE

DO I KNOW A "WALLACE"?
DAD!!
Will Henry

MOM IS GONNA MAKE YOU TAKE OFF THAT PUMPKIN FOR DINNER

HN... Hnggg
HHNGGGG
Heng!
Will Henry

IT'S NOT COMIN' OFF!
MAYBE MOM WON'T NOTICE

Will Henry

THING'S NOT COMIN' OFF
AT LEAST I'LL HAVE AN **EPIC** SCHOOL PHOTO!

UM, HUN, I MAY NEED A HAND WITH AN INCIDENT TAKING PLACE IN THE KITCHEN

WALLACE WAS PLAYIN' AROUND AND GOT HIS HEAD STUCK IN A PUMPKIN
WHAT?

OH MY GOODNESS !!!
Will Henry

THAT'S ADORABLE
I'M SURE YOU MEANT TO SAY "MENACING"

SO, SHOULD I GRAB THE CHAINSAW ?
WHAT? NO! TRY TO STAY STILL, WALLACE
NO, DAD!

JUST GIVE IT A LITTLE TWIST AND-
PULL
William Henry

POP

OOFF, YOU OK?
I FEEL NAKED

WALLACE!!
C'MON DOWNSTAIRS SO WE CAN SEE YOUR COSTUME!
grumble FINE
Will Henry

HOW CUTE! OH, WALLACE, I AM SO GLAD YOU WENT WITH MY CRAYON IDEA!!
CRAYON

HA! LEMME GRAB THE CAMERA!
MOM DON'T.

WAY TO TAKE ONE FOR THE TEAM, WALLACE...
NEXT YEAR, MUTANT ZOMBIE HUNTER!
what flavor are you?

WAIT, YOU'RE BOTH COMING?
YES! DAD DRIVES THE TRUCK AND I SIT IN THE BACK WITH YOU KIDS

MOM... WHO'S GONNA PASS OUT CANDY?!?
DON'T WORRY! I'M LEAVING A BOWL OF CANDY ON THE DECK

SO EACH TRICK-OR-TREATER CAN TAKE A SINGLE PIECE
OPEN YOUR EYES, MOM!!
Take one
Will Henry

EVERYBODY READY FOR SOME TRICK-OR-TREATING?
WAIT, I'M COMIN'!

WHAT'RE YOU SUPPOSED TO BE... THE MOON?
I'M THE ASTEROID THAT KILLED THE DINOSAURS

OOOOOH SPOOKY
YOU'LL THANK ME WHEN YOU'RE **NOT** EATEN BY A VELOCIRAPTOR
Will Henry

WOW, AMELIA... YOU'RE A PRINCESS?!
ECK DON'T REMIND ME!!
Will Henry

EVERY YEAR MY MOM'S LIKE, "OH, AMELIA, BE A PRINCESS, IT WOULD MAKE ME SO HAPPY BLAH BLAH BLAH"

I THINK YOU LOOK NICE!
COMIN' FROM THE KIDNEY STONE!

I WOULD CALL YOUR COSTUME MORE QUAINT THAN LAME
IT'S **LAME**, **SPUD!!** AND I WISH I COULD MAKE IT COOLER
Will Henry

I SHOULD WRITE A COMIC BOOK ABOUT A HALF-CRAYON, HALF-HUMAN SUPERHERO...

THE CRAYON
LEAVING A PERMANENT MARK ON CRIME!
KRA KOOM!
CRAYON

FIGHTING FOR TRUTH, JUSTICE, AND CERULEAN BLUE!
SOUNDS **TOO** VIOLENT FOR ME

TRICK OR TREAT!!
OH HOW LOVELY!

WAIT... WHAT ARE THESE?

RAISINS!?
Crunch

THIS WAND IS A WEAPON!
TIME TO GO!
Will Henry

-Spud

-Spud

ZIP

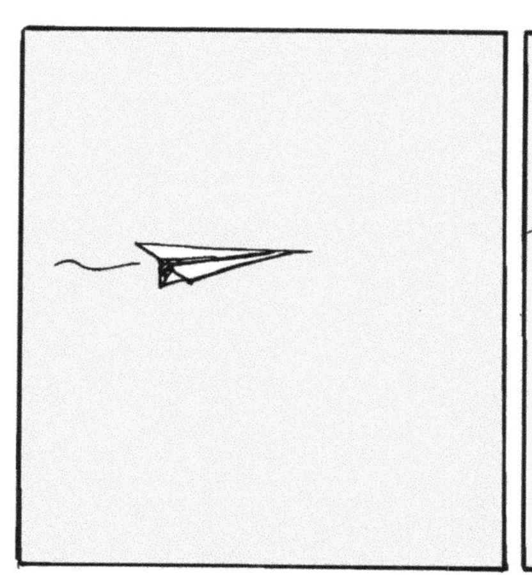

ZIPPY-DO

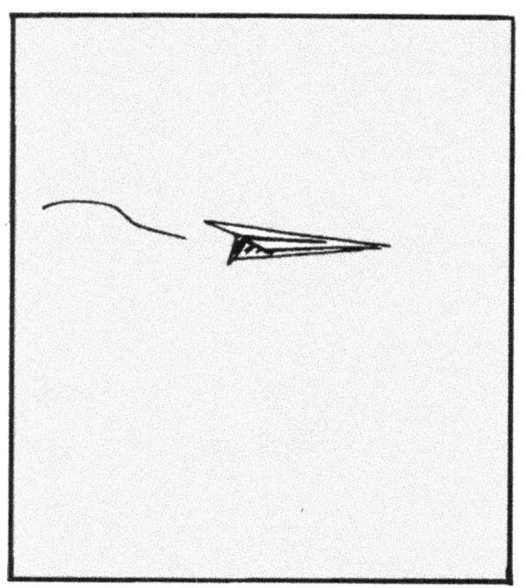

!
ZIP

WHADDAYA GOT THERE, WALLACE?
hm?

OH RIGHT, MY DAD PACKED LUNCH...

A PINEAPPLE IN A SHOPPING BAG?
HE'S STILL GETTING THE HANG OF IT
WillHenry

WALLACE, WE'VE BEEN TRUDGING THROUGH THE GOONIE GRASS ALL MORNING

AND HONESTLY
Will Henry

I THINK WE'RE LOST!
PROBABLY, I'VE BEEN FOLLOWIN' THIS BUTTERFLY

SPUD, TODAY'S THE DAY SOMEONE SAYS "HEY, LOOK HOW COOL AND RADICAL SPUD IS"
what?

STAND UP TALL AND MIGHTY AND LOOK THE WORLD DEAD IN THE EYE...
THIS FEELS WEIRD, WALLACE

AND STRUT WITH CONFIDENCE !!!
I'M GOIN' FOR IT!!

WHAT HAPPENED ?
PULLED SOMETHIN'
William Henry

FOR MY SCIENCE PROJECT, I STARTED MIXING PLANT FERTILIZER WITH MY SHAMPOO

IN THREE WEEKS I'M HOPING TO HAVE A FULL GARDEN, COMPLETE WITH A MEMORIAL BENCH AND CERAMIC GNOME
!
Will "the giraffe boy" Henry

HERE'S A PASS, GO SEE THE NURSE
THUS REVOLUTIONIZING THE WIG INDUSTRY
Hall PASS

THIS IS THE TREE YOU WANT A TIRE SWING ON?
MAKE SURE IT'S HIGH UP
Will Henry

WHERE'D YOU GET THIS GRIMY OLD TIRE ANYWAY?
PULLED IT UP WITH A LOBSTER TRAP
Twirl

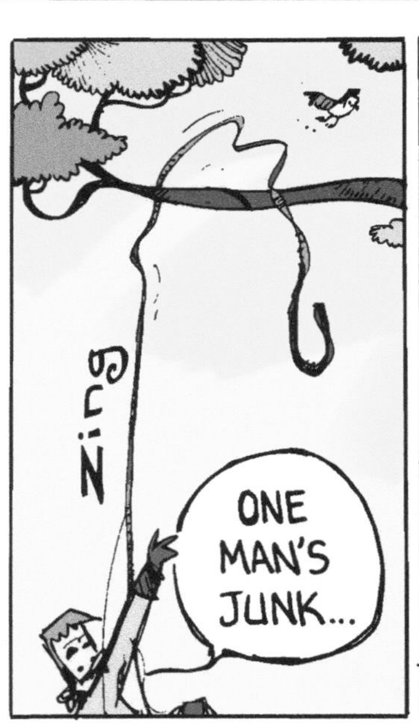
Zing
ONE MAN'S JUNK...

...IS ANOTHER MAN'S JUNK TIED TO A PIECE OF ROPE

Boing
Boing
Boing

Will Henry

LOOKS GOOD ENOUGH TO ME
WHEN DO THE ENGINEERS GET HERE?

YOU KIDS HAVE **TWO** OPTIONS ON THE TIRE SWING

I CAN EITHER **SPIN** YOU TO THE POINT OF NAUSEA...
Will Henry

OR **SLING** YOU SO **HIGH** YOU MIGHT LOSE OXYGEN
Zing

SLING!!
SPIN!
IS THERE A DOOR NUMBER THREE?

WHEN IS THIS STUPID EGG SUPPOSED TO HATCH?!
I HOPE IT'S A PUFFIN

PUFFINS ARE NON-THREATENING
I HOPE IT'S SOME CRAZY RARE PARROT FROM THE AMAZON
GUTEN TAG!
Will Henry

THAT SPEAKS FLUENT GERMAN
I HOPE IT'S AN ALLIGATOR

WALLACE, I GOT YOU A NEW SWEATER WITH A BRONTOSAURUS ON IT! PRETTY NEAT, HUH?

MOM, I HATE TO BE THE BEARER OF BAD NEWS, BUT-
Will Henry

THEY'RE NOT EVEN SURE IF THERE EVER WAS A BRONTO-SAURUS
IT WAS AN APATOSAURUS
I'M NOT RETURNING THE SWEATER

DAD, DO YOU EVER GET TIRED OF USING THE WOOD STOVE?
HA! NEVER
Will Henry

IT'S COZY, IT'S EFFICIENT, BUT Y'KNOW WHAT THE BEST PART IS?

IT LOOKS LIKE A GIANT TIKI HEAD?
KEEPS MY COCOA WARM

Foosh
DAD, I DON'T KNOW WHY YOU STILL USE YOUR RECORD PLAYER

WE CAN GET YOU A DEVICE THE SIZE OF A CHICLET THAT CAN HOLD MORE SONGS THAN YOU'VE EVER HEARD!
actual size
W. Henry

BUT, INSTEAD, YOU HAVE TO GET UP EVERY TWO SECONDS TO FLIP SIDES!

IT KEEPS YOU YOUNG
I'M SO SICK OF BEING YOUNG

HEY LOOK! THE FIRST SNOWFLAKE OF THE SEASON!

WOOOOW

Will Henry

SURE IS TAKIN' ITS SWEET TIME

THERE IT IS
BLACKBERRY HILL, MY TICKET TO THE FUTURE

CORRECT, YOU SHOULD BE ABLE TO GAIN ENOUGH SPEED TO INSTANTLY TRAVEL FORWARD THROUGH TIME

DO YOU HAVE YOUR SUPPLIES?
YEP, WATER, MATCHES, BUTTER KNIFE

GOOD, BECAUSE CHANCES ARE IT'S GONNA BE A BLEAK, DESOLATE WASTELAND, OVERRUN BY ALIEN-MUTANT HYBRIDS
ZZZT!
BOOM

AND ONCE YOU GET THERE, I **NEED** YOU TO FIND ME, WALLACE...

AND SEE IF I EVER OPENED THAT QUAINT B+B
YOUR **DREAM**, SPUD!

MAHM!! CAN I WEAR MY DR. SEUSS HAT TO THANKS-GIVING ?!?

hm, YOU WEARING CLEAN SOCKS?
yes
Will Henry

CLEAN UNDERWEAR ?
yes

ROCK IT, KIDDO
A **WIN** FOR STYLE

FINALLY! I FINALLY FOUND AN AWESOME HIDE-AND-SEEK SPOT!

HA HA THEY'RE GONNA BE LOOKIN' FOR ME ALL RECESS
Billy Henry

I DON'T KNOW WHY I DIDN'T THINK OF THIS BEFORE

IT'S GENIUS

YOU KNOW WHY I DON'T LIKE BEING UP HERE, WALLACE?

WE'LL BE THE FIRST TO GET RAINED ON
yeah

I WAS GONNA SAY "YOUR CRIPPLING FEAR OF HEIGHTS"
OH, THAT TOO
Will Henry

Will Henry
CARS & CHEEP
$$$
BUY

I KNOW WHAT I WANT FOR CHRISTMAS

oh Christmas tree, oh

?
RUSTLE
rustle

RARRL
!
Foosh
pop

STERLING, YOU ARE COVERED IN SAP
so are you!
Will Henry

WHY HELLO, LITTLE BOY! WHAT WOULD YOU LIKE FOR CHRISTMAS?
HI, SANTA! I WANT A CELL PHONE THIS YEAR

HO HO HO! A CELL PHONE?
YES, SANTA, A REALLY BIG CELL PHONE!

OK, YOU GOT-
SO BIG, THAT PEOPLE SAY-

"HEY, IS THAT KID TALKIN' TO A BOOGIE BOARD?"
:GASP: this one reeks like cheese
W. Henry

SANTA, I WOULD LIKE A WILLIAMS BRAND FUNHOUSE PINBALL MACHINE WITH-

WAIT!

DO I HAVE TO OFFICIALLY **ASK** FOR PEACE ON EARTH?
Will Henry

OR IS IT SORT OF IMPLIED?
YOU'D BE SURPRISED, KID

SANTA, DOES RUDOLPH'S NOSE GET **SO** HOT...

ZZZZTT
IT TURNS INTO A LASER?!
Will Henry

WHY DO YOU THINK HE'S AT THE FRONT OF THE SLEIGH?
YOU'VE WEAPONIZED CHRISTMAS

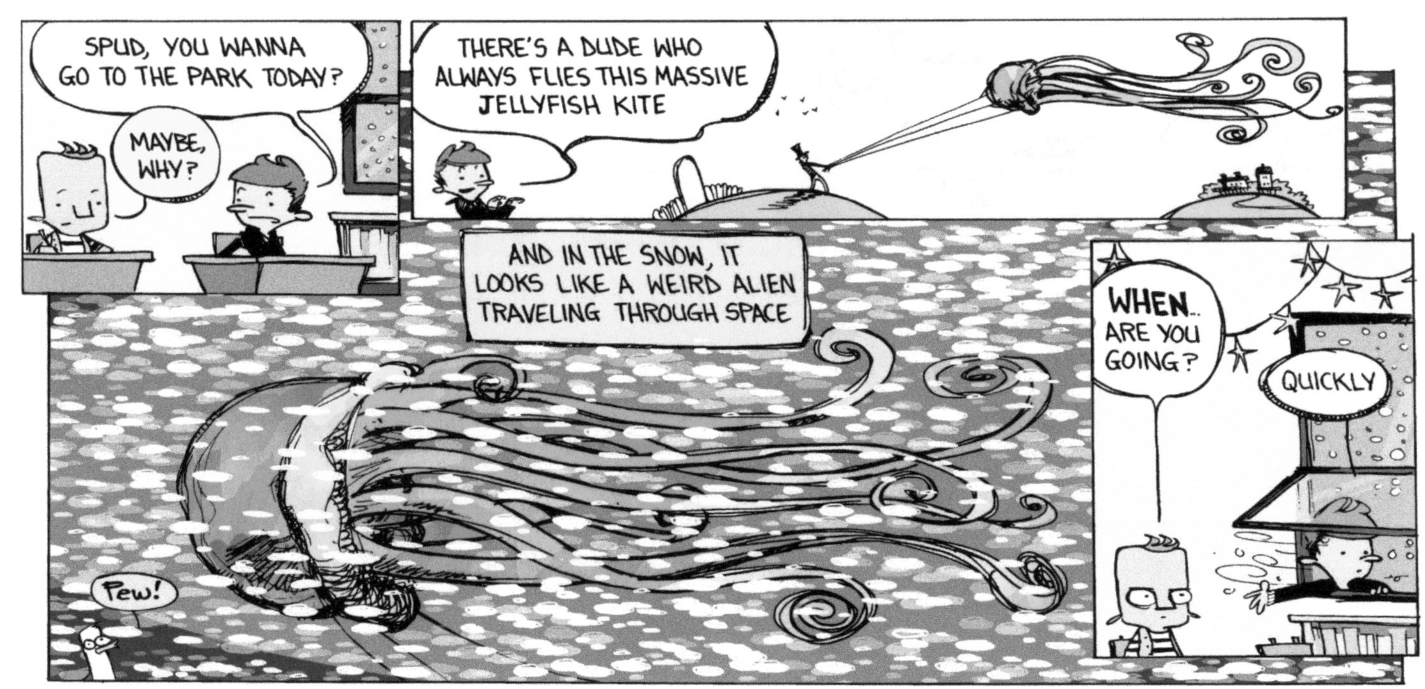
SPUD, YOU WANNA GO TO THE PARK TODAY?
MAYBE, WHY?
THERE'S A DUDE WHO ALWAYS FLIES THIS MASSIVE JELLYFISH KITE
AND IN THE SNOW, IT LOOKS LIKE A WEIRD ALIEN TRAVELING THROUGH SPACE
Pew!
WHEN... ARE YOU GOING?
QUICKLY

IT'S COLD OUT
IF YOU WANNA FLY A KITE, GO OUTSIDE
Will "hi, mom!" Henry

HERE, WALLACE
WHAT'S THIS?
THE NARWHAL
Snug Harbor, RI

YOU'VE ALWAYS WANTED A PET
A BARNACLE ?

WANT TWO PETS?
THAT'S NOT FUNNY
THE NARWHAL
Snug Harbor, RI
Will Henry

ONE OF THESE DAYS I'M GONNA GET OUTTA SCHOOL...
...RUN DOWN THE HILL TO THE DOCKS...
...HOP ON THE **FIRST** BOAT I SEE AND EXPLORE THE WORLD
Will Henry

YOU IN?
SOUNDS LIKE A LOT OF RUNNING

WHOA! SPUD, YOU GOT A DRONE FOR CHRIST-MAS?!
YEP, YOU SHOULD GET ONE TOO, WALLACE
ZZzZ
W. Henry

FOOSH

FOR HOVER SHOES...
FOR WHEN YOU BREAK MINE

I THINK MY EYEBALLS ARE STARTING TO FREEZE
LOOK! YOU CAN SEE YOUR BREATH!

hhaaaaaaa
Will Henry

SMELLS LIKE YOU HAD A GOOD BREAK-FAST
SARDINE OMELETTE

MY DAD IS PULLING UP LOBSTER TRAPS TODAY, IF YOU WANNA COME
WALLACE, YOU **KNOW** I DON'T LIKE GOIN' ON BOATS
Will Henry

IT'S TOO HARD TO EAT SOUP
BRING A STRAW

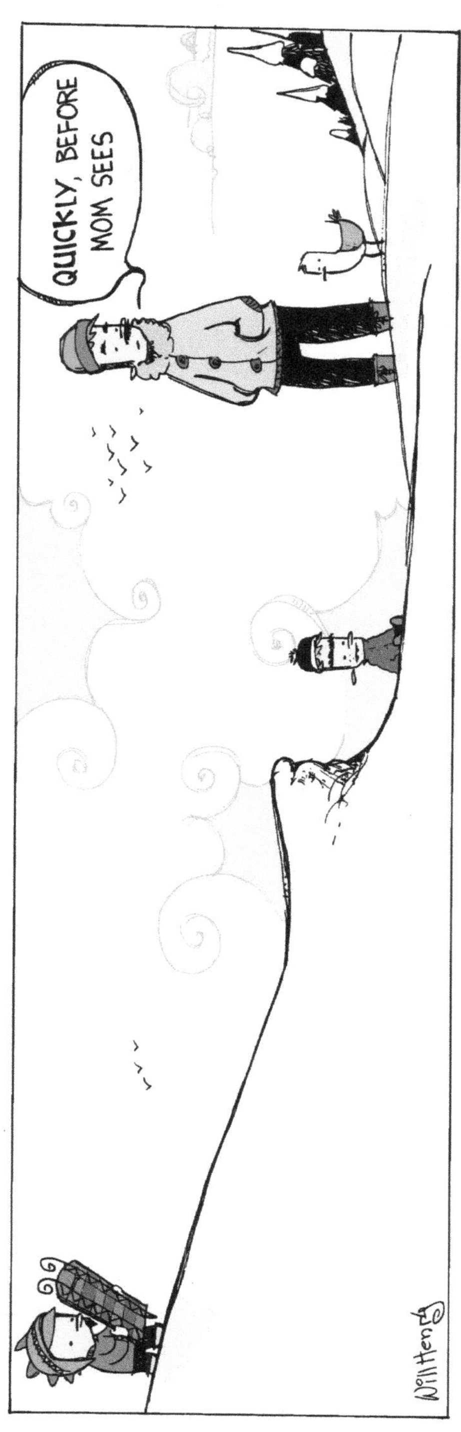
QUICKLY, BEFORE MOM SEES

I HAVE A THEORY ABOUT SEAWEED
WHICH IS?

EVERY MONTH, THE ROYAL BARBER HAS TO TRIM KING TRITON'S ARM-PIT HAIR
how's the fam?

The ATLA

YECK! SEAWEED IS REGAL ARM-PIT HAIR?
THAT'S WHY IT IS SO MUCH FUN TO PLAY WITH

I LEFT SOME OLD GORGONZOLA IN MY DESK OVER THE WEEKEND

W. Henry
WHAT ARE THE CHANCES IT'S EVOLVED INTO SOME SENTIENT BEING, HUNGRY FOR HUMAN FLESH?
feed me!

YOU NEED TO DUCT TAPE THAT DESK SHUT IMMEDIATELY
SO, I SHOULDN'T EAT IT?

WHAT'VE YOU GOT THERE, WALLACE?
MRS. MACINTOSH GAVE ME SOME CARROT SEEDS FOR MY GARDEN
W. Henry

I'LL PLANT THEM, AND AFTER A FEW MONTHS, WITH A LITTLE LOVE AND CARE, I'LL HAVE CARROTS!
Carrots

I **GUESS** THAT'S COOL...

Y'KNOW THEY SELL CARROTS AT THE MARKET?
THEY DO?

WALLACE, CAN YOU PLEASE READ FROM PAGE TWO IN YOUR BOOK?
YES, MA'AM
GOLD STAR

SHWAPS KICKS DOWN THE DOOR-BAM!
"WE MEET AGAIN, PROFESSOR PORPOISE, PREPARE FOR-"

cricket
cricket
?
?
?
?
?
W. Henry

OH, YOU MEAN THE BOOK YOU'RE ALL READING?
Shwaps

IT'S NIGHTS LIKE THESE THAT MAKE ME THINK...
Will Henry

HOW **AWESOME** IT WOULD BE TO HAVE A JETPACK
OR A CUBAN ON RYE

GEORGE WASHINGTON KNEW HE WAS NO MATCH FOR THE ROBO-REDCOATS
not today you bolts of Brit!

HE LEAPED FROM THE CARGO HATCH, BUT NOT BEFORE PRESSING-
Click

THE DETONATOR!
BA-BOOM

AND IF NOT FOR A HEROIC BALD EAGLE,

OL' GEORGE NEVER WOULD HAVE HAD A MOST AWESOME IDEA

HIS IDEA WAS... AMERICA
I SAID **NON**-FICTION, NOT **FAN** FICTION
GOLD STA

PsSs/t
SPUD, YOU WANT A ROOT BEER BARREL?
ABSOLUTELY

THANKS, WALLACE

I FOUND A BUNCH OF 'EM IN THE PARKING LOT
I NEED TO GO TO THE NURSE
Will Henry
2/13

I WANNA GIVE AMELIA A VALENTINE, BUT I DON'T KNOW WHAT TO WRITE

AND IF I DON'T WORD IT JUST RIGHT, SHE MAY STRIKE ME

KEEP IT SIMPLE AND FROM THE HEART

Pizza ROCKS!
XOXO-SPUD
Will Henry

GOODBYE, COMMANDER CATACLYSM
Happy Birthday

Happy Birthday
Will Henry

AND GOOD LUCK ON YOUR JOURNEY TO THE MOON
I'VE PREPARED SOME WORDS

CLASS, IN THIS BROWN BAG I HAVE A RATHER SPECIAL ST. PATRICK'S DAY SURPRISE!
I LOVE SURPRISES

THIS MORNING I CAPTURED A REAL, LIVE...
Will Henry

LEPRECHAUN!!!
WH OOOAAA
gasp
BOOM

AND IF YOU'RE WELL BEHAVED, I'LL SHOW HIM TO YOU AT THE END OF THE DAY
AND THERE'S THE CATCH

CAN YOU BELIEVE MRS. MACINTOSH CAPTURED A LEPRECHAUN ???
I DON'T UNDER-STAND LEPRE-CHAUNS

YOU'RE TELLIN' ME THERE'S LITTLE GREEN ELF THINGS RUNNIN' AROUND YELLING -
OH EY, MON! YA NEHVA GWAN GIT MAH GOALD
Willy Henry

WHHHYY WOULD IT HAVE A JAMAICAN ACCENT?
WHY NOT?! NONE OF IT MAKES SENSE ANYWAY!!

I'VE ALWAYS WANTED TO SEE A LEPRECHAUN, SPUD
munch munch

AND TO THINK, MRS. MACINTOSH ACTUALLY CAUGHT ONE AND IS KEEPING IT IN THAT BAG ON HER DESK!

it's haunting me, Spud!

I'M TOO DISTRACTED TO FINISH THIS MACARONI PORTRAIT
CAN I TAKE YOUR MACARONI HOME?
munch
W. Henry

MRS. MACINTOSH CAUGHT A LEPRECHAUN, A REAL LEPRECHAUN!

HOW BIG IS IT? DOES IT HAVE GOLD? IS IT MAGICAL? I'M LOSING IT!
Will Henry

IT'S ALL I CAN THINK ABOUT! I-HAVE-TO-SEE-THIS-LEPRECH-

ANYTIME NOW, WALLACE
HOW DID I GET UP HERE?

MRS. MACINTOSH, IT'S ALMOST THE END OF THE DAY. CAN WE SEE THE LEPRECHAUN?
I SUPPOSE, LET ME JUST...
GOLD STAR

WAIT A MINUTE...

OH MY WORD!
Gasp

what have you done ?
TAKE A BREATH

WALLACE, CAN YOU PLEASE, PLEASE FOCUS AND HELP ME FIND YOUR BOOTS ?!?
MOM MOM
CAN I WEAR MY POLKA-DOT SHIRT?

WALLACE, YOU CAN LITERALLY WEAR WHATEVER YOU WANT AS LONG AS YOU FIND YOUR BOOTS AND GET TO THE BLASTED BUS ON TIME !!!
Will Henry

I FOUND A LOOP-HOLE

WALLACE, C'MON, IT'S TIME FOR DINNER
RIGHT NOW?!

I WANNA WATCH THIS SPIDER FINISH SPINNING A WEB
WHERE?

W.Henry

LAST YEAR, I HAD **WAY** LESS RESPONSIBILITIES, SPUD

I'D WAKE UP EARLY AND GET TO CHASE THE GARBAGE TRUCK **ALL MORNING**!
?
hahahaha ha
Will Henry

NOW, I NEVER HAVE TIME FOR MY HOBBIES
I'M **SO** GLAD YOU DON'T DO THAT ANYMORE

WHAT IS THAT, WALLACE ?
I BELIEVE IT'S SOME SASQUATCH SCAT

I FOUND IT ON A VERY SUSPICIOUS GAME TRAIL AND COLLECTED A SAMPLE FOR TESTING
Will Henry

I WAS HOPING IT WAS A JAR OF POO
IT'S PROOF !!!

WHOA, SPUD!

YOU HAVE A TELESCOPE ?!?
MY MOTHER GOT IT FOR ME

THINK OF ALL THE AMAZING STARS AND PLANETS WE'LL BE ABLE TO SEE
it's cool, I Know...
Will Henry

WHAT'RE YOU LOOKIN' AT NOW?
WAIT DON'T

PIZZA
order in
Take out

spud.
DON'T TELL MY MOM

WHERE YOU GUYS GOIN'?
TRUSTOM POND

WE'RE GONNA HAVE A MELLOW DAY COLLECTING MUSHROOMS AND CATCHING NEWTS
Will Henry

WE'RE ALSO TRACKING A GIANT CRETACEOUS PERIOD SNAPPING TURTLE NAMED GRAMPS!!

THAT'S NOT WHAT YOU TOLD ME ON THE PHONE
I DIDN'T MENTION THAT?

YOUR NET LOOKS PRETTY BEAT UP, WALLACE
OH, RIGHT
Will Henry

I TRIED TO CATCH A SEAGULL LAST WEEK...

LESSON LEARNED

YOU GUYS REMEMBER WHEN FARMER BROWN'S COW DISAPPEARED ?

SOME PEOPLE BELIEVE GRAMPS **DEVOURED IT**!!
wha?
moo ?
Mooo

WHAT PEOPLE BELIEVE THAT ?
MOSTLY ME

THIS IS A GOOD PLACE TO LURE OUT GRAMPS

SPUD, TOSS IN SOME OF THE STALE BREAD I BROUGHT
I **CAN'T**, WALLACE

I GOT NERVOUS AND ATE IT...
Will Henry

I THOUGHT IT WAS A GIANT CROUTON
Spud
YOUR **FACE** IS A CROUTON

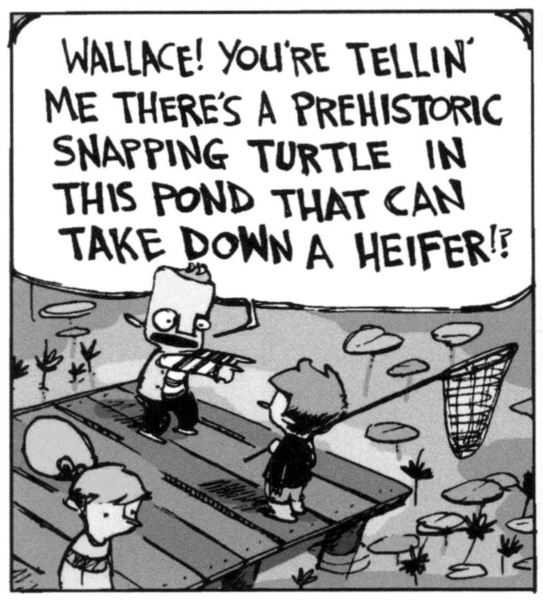
WALLACE! YOU'RE TELLIN' ME THERE'S A PREHISTORIC SNAPPING TURTLE IN THIS POND THAT CAN TAKE DOWN A HEIFER!?

AND YOU'VE BROUGHT ME OUT HERE TO CAPTURE IT!?!
Will Henry

SPUD! IT'S OK!
huff huff huff

I HAVE A BUTTERFLY NET
MIGHT AS WELL BE A TOOTH-PICK

I WAS PLANNING ON USING BREAD TO LURE THE SNAPPER OUT

BUT SINCE **SOMEONE** ATE ALL THE BREAD...
NO REGRETS

I'LL HAVE TO USE **LIVE** BAIT
REGRETS
SPLASH
SPLASH
SPLASH

C'MON, GRAMPS, YOU BIG, BEAUTIFUL TURTLE. I KNOW YOU'RE -
SPLASH
SPLASH

out there

Will Henry

WE'RE GONNA NEED A BIGGER NET

WALLACE, THIS ISN'T A SNAPPING TURTLE. THIS IS A DINOSAUR!!

I DARE YOU TO TOUCH IT
WHAT?

YEAH, FLICK ITS SHELL, TOUGH GUY
I BET I COULD RIDE IT LIKE A BOOGIE BOARD
TAKE ME NOW, MOTHER NATURE!
Will Henry

SPUD, LOOK AT THE SIZE OF THIS SNAPPING TURTLE!!
I'M NOT LOOKING, WALLACE!

SPUD, LOOK! I'M GONNA TRY AND TOUCH IT
I'M WALKING AWAY

SPUD, LOOK
NO!

splash
Will Henry

SPUD
WALLACE, GEMME OUTTA HERE!!!

SPUD! YOU OK?!?
I DUNNO! DID THE TURTLE GET ME?

DO I HAVE ALL MY FINGERS ?!?
Phew
Will Henry

TAKE A BREATH, BUDDY
TEN! IS THAT RIGHT ?!?

ARE YOU GONNA BE OKAY, SPUD?
huff huff OH MY GOSH, huff I THINK I NEED CPR

huff huff

FROM AMELIA
oh, Boy
Will Henry

Splash

GAH, WALLACE, I'M SO EMBARRASSED
SPUD! WHAT'RE YOU TALKIN' ABOUT ?

YOU SWAM WITH THE BEAST, MY FRIEND!

YOU'RE GONNA BE A HERO, MAN
hero?
NOT IF I TELL PEOPLE WHAT REALLY HAPPENED

YOU SHUT YOUR EYES AND WALKED OFF A DOCK
YOU DID IT WITH YOUR EYES CLOSED!!
Will "mr. Quahog" Henry

WHY WON'T YOU GO IN THE OCEAN, SPUD?
BECAUSE, WALLACE!
I WOULD BE "THAT KID" WHO GETS SWALLOWED BY A BLUE WHALE

I'D END UP LIVING IN ITS BELLY, EATING BARNACLES AND SOCIALIZING WITH INANIMATE OBJECTS
you really hurt my feelings, Bryan...

ONLY TO EMERGE YEARS LATER, DEPRAVED AND UNRECOGNIZABLE
MAYBE YOU WOULDN'T WANT YOUR MOTHER TO RECOGNIZE YOU
SHE'D HAVE ME MAKE UP **YEARS** OF PIANO LESSONS

YOU GUYS WANT PENCIL TOPPERS?
FOR REALZIES !?!

YOU'RE GIVING THEM AWAY?!
Will Henry

SURE, WHY NOT?
THAT'S REALLY COOL, WALLACE

I GAVE A SEAGULL A FRENCH FRY, ONCE
EASY, MOTHER TERESA

WALLACE, MAYBE I COULD BE AN ASTRONAUT WITH YOU
REALLY?

SURE, THERE ARE SOME NEGATIVES

LIKE MY TETHER SNAPPING AND I SLOWLY DRIFT INTO A LONESOME OBLIVION
SNAP

THE POSITIVES?
I'VE NEVER HAD A TACO IN SPACE

HEY, SPUD, YOU THERE?
KRKK no.

YOU EVER THINK SHOOTING STARS ARE SIMPLY ALIEN DEBRIS...
Will Henry

FROM A GALACTIC WAR FOUGHT EONS AGO?

KRRKK I'M GOING BACK TO BED
IT'S ONLY MID-NIGHT

Grow your own Avocado Plant!

Start with a regular ol' avocado pit, cleaned and wiped dry.

I'm free

Toothpicks

ToothPicks

A clear glass or jar

Locate the top of the avocado pit. The top usually has a tiny point to it.

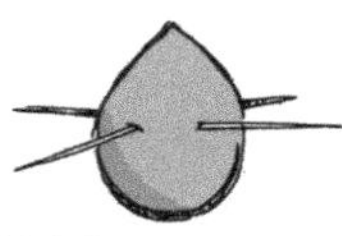

Stick four toothpicks into the avocado pit, like the picture above.

Fill the glass with water, almost to the tippity top.

Place the avocado into the glass so that the toothpicks rest on the rim and the bottom half of the avocado pit sits in the water.

here we go!

After about three weeks, the avocado pit should begin to sprout a tiny, delicate root into the water.

Eventually, the top part will dry out and crack, while the roots continue to grow.

At six to eight weeks, a sprout should emerge from the crack, the start of your very own avocado plant!

Patience!

Make sure to change the water every week, and keep the water level of your glass or jar high enough to submerge the avocado pit.

You look very handsome, Avocado Plant
Why, thank you

After the sprout has grown taller than six inches, remove it from the water glass and plant it in some soil. It's important to give your avocado plant plenty of sunlight and lots of compliments.

I definitely had too much guacamole

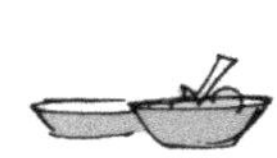

WALLACE'S GUIDE TO KEEPING A

Trust me, I kinda know what I'm talking about.

A field guide is a cool way to keep track of all the hikes and parks you visit. I use a regular ol' spiral notebook, but you can use anything you want, from blank sketchbooks to stapled pieces of computer paper. Whenever I get outside with my field book, I always use one page to describe where I am and the opposite page to tape down all the cool things I find, like ferns, feathers, flowers, and sticks.

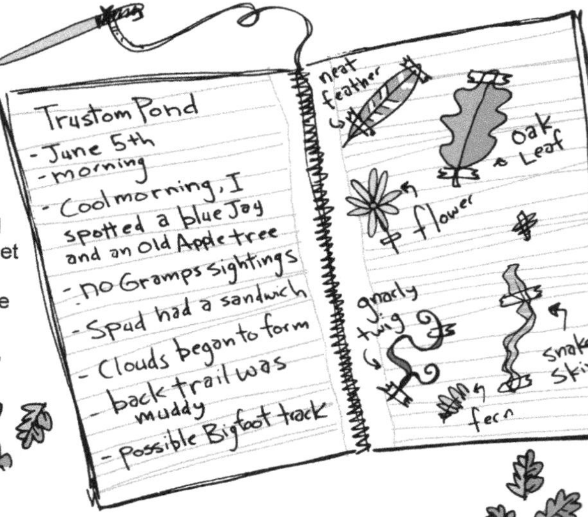

Trustom Pond
- June 5th
- morning
- Cool morning, I spotted a blue Jay and an old Apple tree
- no Gramps sightings
- Spud had a sandwich
- Clouds began to form
- back trail was muddy
- possible Bigfoot track
neat feather
oak Leaf
flower
gnarly twig
snake skin
fern

To keep a good field book, make sure you start each page with the date and time you go on your hikes—it's fun to compare them with the change of seasons. It's also important to have a pen or pencil handy. I tie mine to a string and staple it to the notebook. Staple a resealable plastic bag to the front of your field book to keep bigger objects you find, like neat shells, rocks, and pine cones. It's also where I keep my roll of tape.

Boom! That's it. Super easy, right?! A good outdoors person keeps track of their adventures! All that's left is to get out there and find some interesting things!

Winter Mobile

WHAT YOU'LL NEED

Tupperware

String

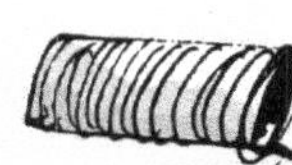

Cool, colorful things you've collected outside, like shells, twigs, leaves, or rocks

Cut the string 2–3 feet long and lay it on the bottom of your Tupperware.

Place your colorful object into the Tupperware on top of the string, and get creative with it!

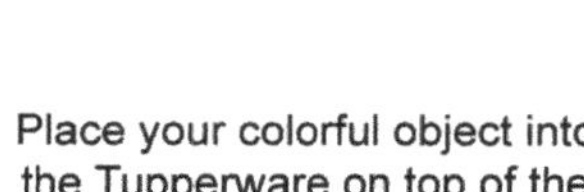

Fill the Tupperware with water just till it covers the objects. It's OK if they float around.

Pop that thing in the freezer, and wait for the water to turn to ice, usually around 2–3 hours depending on the size.

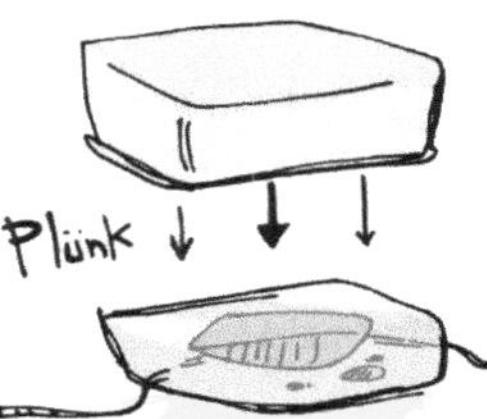

Flip the frozen mobile over and wiggle the Tupperware. The block of ice should fall out.

Now you've got your cool winter mobile.

GET CREATIVE!

Try different sizes of Tupperware and connect them with a single string before you freeze them. This will add more parts to your mobile.

Head outside and hang them in your favorite tree, on your balcony, or in your snow fort.

*Note: Winter mobiles work best on colder days or snow days!

Wallace the Brave is distributed internationally by Andrews McMeel Syndication.

Andrews McMeel Publishing
a division of Andrews McMeel Universal
1130 Walnut Street, Kansas City, Missouri 64106

www.andrewsmcmeel.com

ISBN: 978-1-5248-5581-9

Library of Congress Control Number: 2019932902

Look for these books!